This is a work of fiction. Names, characters, businesses, places, events and incidents are

either the products of the author's imagination or used in a fictitious manner. Any

resemblance to actual persons, living or dead, or actual events is purely coincidental.

Copyright © 2017, Unique Realities

The Order of Flame

Book 2

7

Aparicio's room was stripped, its walls reinforced and then rebuilt. Cameras were then installed in all the rooms to prevent students from having any guests when they were supposed to be sleeping. In the following years Aparicio, Ridha and Kolya trained closely together. Helping the other recruits when they could, they even extended support to Arthur who had quickly declined. Every day they pushed their minds to the limit with problem solving and general knowledge questions. Physical endurance was tested every day with Mr. Quwan who pushed them just as hard mentally with different scenarios in the ever changing gauntlet.

In history class they continued to learn about the history of the Order. Some deeds the Order had done throughout the centuries were just as bad as they were good but each assignment had served a higher purpose. The symbol of the Order of Flame was a large fire ball, hollowed out and shaped almost like the letter 'U' with three small flames, one on top and one on either side of the fire ball.

"The large fire you see here is the Order as a whole," Mr. Reid said in class. "We are not like the other clans. They will typically send one to do an assignment but they are nothing more than petty assassins!" he shouted raising his finger to point at the students. "You are not trained to be petty, you are not just assassins, you are much, much more. Anyone can kill but that's not the point of all this, we train you to be invisible. That's why we send three, to cover one another. So when you see three agents," he said pointing to the three flames around the large flame on the dry erase board. "That's what this means. It means we're never alone."

In etiquette class they learned different forms of dancing, many of which could be adapted to a specific fighting technique. They learned breathing techniques that could be used during their physical training with Mr. Quwan. Professor Kjeldsen made them perfectionists with their appearances, teaching them how to dress properly for any occasion as well as self grooming techniques.

"Sometimes the situation will call for you to get close to your targets. You must know how to think like them, walk and talk like them. You must learn to dress like them and possibly dance like them." she said as she watched the boys and girls pick out matching clothes from a pile thrown onto a table. "Knowing how to dress for an assignment is just as important as knowing how to kill. Mr. Quwan wouldn't teach you to engage in a gunfight with bullets and no pistol. I do not want you to walk into a room wearing sleeping attire when you should be in a suit or dress." she explained as she stopped Kolya from grabbing a blue tie that would have clashed with his black suit.

    Professor Ch'ang had them learn archery which allowed them to reinforce the breathing techniques taught by Professor Kjeldsen. They each had to shoot both stationed and moving targets over a thousand meters away. "We do not always get to choose the perfect time for a strike. There will be times that you will have to take it and your target will be far and silence is the only method in which to make the kill. If that is the case, a bow, can swiftly engage an enemy killing them quickly without so much as a whisper." he said pushing Ridha's feet further apart. "This like anything else is an art,"

As they stood in a row looking at targets ten meters away Mr. Quwan handed them each a Glock .26 pistol and a box of ammunition. As they studied the weapon they all smiled as they knew they would be able to shoot the gun eventually.

"This is the last line of defense and will be carried by all agents in the field." he said showing them how to load the bullets and properly slide the magazine clip into the gun. An entire day was spent teaching them how to properly shoot, disassemble and clean the Glock .26 while other days were broken up to teach them how to use other firearms.

"We teach you to use the area around you to your advantage, but there will be times when you will need sufficient firepower to stop an overwhelming force of individuals. You will be prepared, you will be calm and you will succeed!" Mr. Quwan shouted.

As the students sat in their history class they stared at Mr. Reid as he taught them about their enemies, eight other groups from around the world who were training just as they were.

"We are the Order of Flame, not the oldest group and certainly not the weakest. These are the other clans we know of. In

Egypt there is the Brotherhood of Scorpions. China has the Lone Dragons, while the British have the Hub. We had a peace treaty with the Brothers of Shadow that operate out of Japan but that ended three years ago in Chicago. The Church has the Holy Order of Light while America has the Order of Liberty. We've recently learned rumors about a group known as the Divine and Silent Thunder but we do not know if they are connected to an organization quite like us or the others," Mr. Reid said turning on a projector that sent a picture of a Japanese assassin on the dry erase board.

"This month we will study the art and history of two assassins. The first is a member of the Brotherhood of Shadow, his code name was Blood. A skilled warrior who used two katanas that doubled as whips. Blood met his end in Chicago by another Assassin," Mr. Ried changed the slide and the picture of Latin man in a suit walking in a downtown area appeared on the dry erase board.

"His name is Armando and he too had a codename. Swift Shades and up until three years ago he was considered the best assassin in the world until he too met his end in a gunfight in Chicago," Mr. Reid added beginning his lesson.

Knife throwing became a daily routine just like running. Mr. Quwan and Professor Ch'ang had them practice different knife throwing techniques until their arms were numb and their fingers bled. Even Professor Kjeldsen had given them a lesson or two about certain techniques for close quarter combat. When Aparicio and his friends reached the age of nineteen they had mastered knife throws, close quarter combat, mixed martial arts, table etiquette, various forms of dancing, how to hold their breath for up to five minutes, Archery and parkour.

The only thing left to teach them were driving techniques and so for the first time in over eight years the students were allowed to leave the compound they had called home and train in a closed parking lot near the beach.

"Have you ever wondered where in the world we are?" Kolya asked as they stood in line waiting for Mr. Quwan to address them.

"If those exceptionally beautiful women on the beach are any indication then I'd say we are in America," Ridha whispered back.

"You mean those half naked women frolicking in the water?" Aparicio whispered, barely able to contain himself.

"How can you tell?" Kolya asked. "Weren't we told woman swim like that all the time?"

"The men are wearing large baggy trunks rather than Speedos," Ridha laughed and both Kolya and Aparicio's nodded in agreement.

"Where in America is the real question,"

"San Francisco," Aparicio answered and Kolya agreed.

"How can you two tell?" Ridha asked looking around for a clue as Mr. Quwan approached them.

"Look at the license plate on the cars," Aparicio grunted before Mr. Quwan was within earshot.

"Today we learn basic driving techniques, tomorrow we learn advanced driving and the day after we learn evasive driving techniques. Learn these skills quickly, in the following days the weather will not be favorable and this lot will not be available to us," Mr. Quwan said walking the students to the first car.

Time melted away for the students until word was getting around that they were nearing completion of their training. As the months rolled by they were allowed more time out of the school but Mr. Quwan did not make it easy for them. Taking them to the ocean at night where they were told to swim five hundred yards around two buoys before swimming back to shore where they had to throw a knife at two stationary targets and shoot three moving targets then run five hundred yards around two check points. All of this had to be completed five times in less than 80 minutes.

If their guns became water logged, they failed. If they missed a knife throw, they failed if they did not complete the task in less than 80 minutes they failed and failing was not an option. When the time came to quit all the recruits collapsed to the sand gasping for breath while Mr. Quwan stood over them.

"It's not over yet you lazy pieces of shit!" he screamed. "I need a hundred pushups out of you before you can even think of going home!" his scream was even more deafening than the sound of lighting that echoed overhead.

"We have to hurry," Kolya said helping Ridha up.

"I've got nothing left guys," Ridha huffed.

"It's raining Ridha," Aparicio said starting his pushups. "The rain will make it hard to do these pushups in the sand. The faster we do it the quicker we'll be done,"

Ridha nodded his head and began doing his pushups between Aparicio and Kolya.

"It's almost over, isn't it?" Ridha asked.

"Never. It's never over," Kolya whispered.

8

She stared at a picture of her friends for what felt like an eternity before placing it back in an old shoebox. Taking a deep breath she placed the shoebox among the many others in her luxurious walk in closet before exiting wearing a sexy red negligee she had received as a gift from her lover. As she stepped out into the bedroom she smiled at, Ambrogino Colombo.

"You were looking into the shoebox again weren't you," Ambrogino whispered from the center of the queen size bed.

"Unlike you, I've chosen to remember the past," she said approaching the foot of the bed. Slowly she put one foot on the edge of the bed while opening her negligee so that her lover could see her naked body more clearly.

"Will you remember your husband after he's dead?" Ambrogino asked somberly and when she nodded he felt compelled to ask. "What will you remember?"

"I will remember the day he took me off the streets of Spain. I will remember the abuse he dealt when I refused his affections and I will remember the joy I feel when I plunge a knife into his back," she said with a heavy Spanish accent. Ambrogino laughed as he crawled toward her like a lion ready to pounce.

"I had to make sure you weren't starting to have regrets about the plan," he said kissing her inner thigh.

"My only regret will be that you did not take me before my husband comes home," she whispered. Ambrogino quickly grabbed her by the waist and threw her on the bed beside him.

"I like to devour my prey slowly but I see you leave me little choice," he said crawling on top her.

"This prey wants to be devoured whole," she whispered back before biting down on his neck.

After an hour of passionate love making Maria collapsed beside Ambrogino glistening with sweat. While she tried catching her breath Ambrogino had already controlled his breathing before looking over at her.

"Epic," she giggled as he smiled back at her.

"Your husband will be home soon, should we go over the plan one final time?" he asked just before sliding out of the bed to dress himself.

"I wish you wouldn't rush to leave after we've had sex," she said as he retrieved his underwear from beneath the bed. She could not help but admire his slim muscular build and his thick black, hair she had just ran her fingers through.

"That's not what I asked you Maria," Ambrogino said calmly but with enough seriousness that let Maria know he was in no mood for childish banter. Maria sat up from the bed holding a thin sheet to cover her breasts, flipping her long and curly black hair to the side.

"My part is simple, I convince Christopher to hire extra security for the girls that are coming in from Russia." Maria said, her breathing becoming steadier as she continued to watch him dress.

"It isn't so simple, Maria. Christopher is a hard man to convince, you may have to do things that you would otherwise shy away from," Ambrogino turned to her as he covered the abs she loved so much with his black turtle neck sweater. "If he does not listen to you then I cannot do my part,"

"My Love, he will listen to me. Once you hire the assassins to kill the Russians everything will fall into place," Maria said with a wicked smile.

"Why bother covering yourself with a blanket? I've already seen you naked," he asked.

"Because," she said standing up, wrapping the sheet around her body. "The only way for you to undress me, is for me to have something on in the first place," she said arching her eyebrow while motioning from him to come closer. Ambrogino walked closer, placing his hands on her hips.

"Are you ready to be the Queen of Christopher's empire?" he whispered in her ear.

"I am already the Queen, Ambrogino, the question is you ready to be my King?" she asked placing her hands on the sides of his face, the sheet previously wrapped around her body dropping to the side as she kissed him softly on the lips.

Later that day Christopher Fraga watched his wife swim in their pool while body guards stood around keeping watch. Looking down at her beautiful body as it moved underwater like the exotic animal she was had gotten him a little more than excited. Shaking his head he took a deep breath and walked away from the pool to the small table near the house. Soon he would be conducting business and it wouldn't be appropriate for him to do so with an erection. Just as he neared the table, Angela Ostrovsky, his personal body guard stepped out the house.

Her tight black shirt and blue jeans would have been a normal distraction for any man with the exception that her bulging veins were visible through her clothes. A former body builder and ex-Russian soldier, the six foot tall Angela was a force to be reckoned with while a much shorter individual wearing proper Miami clothing stood behind her.

"Phillip," Christopher said with a smile, his arms extended.

"Fucking Miami heat!" he shouted back touching his white t-shirt and cargo shorts. "I wanted to wear a suit but I'd just sweat right though it," Phillip said shaking Christopher's hand.

"It happens. Heat wave for the past three days," Christopher said motioning for Phillip to have a seat at the table. Phillip took a seat at the table while looking Christopher up and down. Today Christopher had donned loose fitting white pants and a bright blue shirt.

"Not to you though. You Miami guys and your bright colors scares the hell out of me more than your body guard," Phillip said looking past Christopher to see

Angela looking more like a golem as she stood behind Christopher.

Smiling back at Phillip, Christopher, asked. "Can I get you anything to drink? Angela can get you anything you'd like from the bar,"

"No, I don't plan on being here long." Phillip said.

"Okay, straight to business then," Christopher said. Maria, having noticed Christopher talking to Phillip swam to the edge of the pool and slowly stepped out. Walking casually to her beach chair she took a seat and reclined it all the way back to do some sunbathing. Grabbing the MP3 player on the side of the chair she placed the headphones in her ear, pretending to listen to music when in actuality she was listening in on Christopher's conversation through a little device placed under the table where the two men sat.

"Okay we have one large shipping container coming into the San Francisco port next week," Phillip said. "You're picking up container 8178, the merchandise inside is well looked after and should stay that way until you come back to Miami,"

"Should?" Christopher said looking more than displeased.

"We wanted to come into the Miami port but we lost those connections which is why you're getting a discount on such high end merchandise. Be grateful, all you have to do is transport everything to Miami but do it quickly and make as few stops as possible." Phillip said.

"What time do I have to be there?" Christopher asked motioning for Angela to lean close.

"2.am sharp and you have to be gone before 3:15," Phillip said as Christopher whispered to Angela. Nodding her head she slowly removed herself from their sight walking back into the house.

"Awfully small time table, what if there are complications?"

"See to it that there are no complications, Chris. At 3:45 we have MS-13 members moving in to pick up a shipment of drugs and guns. If the Russians don't do this quick it could open up suspicions from the port authorities," Phillip said glancing past Christopher to see his wife Maria lying down near the pool.

"I thought you had bought time for the port authorities to look the other way while we conducted our transaction," Christopher asked looking perturbed.

"Look Chris, the economy is shot to shit which makes it easier for guys like us to do what we gotta do. But you never know who's going to have a change in heart at the last minute and try to do the right thing," Phillip said easing Christopher's concern just as Angela arrived with a silver suitcase. Placing the suitcase on the table she slid it towards Phillip.

"As agreed, two million up front. You'll get the rest once I've seen the merchandise in San Francisco," Christopher said as Phillip checked the contents inside the case.

"Okay, we are all good then. You really going to be there for the exchange?" Phillip asked with an arched brow. "Most big bosses don't like getting their hands dirty,"

"I enjoy it very much," Christopher said standing up from the table. Phillip rose and shook his hand.

"See you in a week," he said walking back into the house, Angela following closely. Christopher reached into his pocket and grabbed his phone when Maria approached from behind and gave him a hug.

"Are you done with your business dealings?" she asked.

"No," he said dialing a number.

"You promised to take me shopping," she pouted while taking the seat where Phillip had sat prior.

"Go without me," he said placing the phone to his ear. She took a deep breath as she compared him for the millionth time to Ambrogino. While Christopher was just shy of five foot eight he had the ability to seem larger than life when he spoke, often through intimidation. He was your typical blond hair blue eyed man with a decent sense in fashion. What he lacked in size below his waste he made up for in business.

Ambrogino, her Italian body guard, however was a darker more shadowy figure. His height of six feet and his soft black hair were just as intoxicating as his deep voice. With such an endowed penis and lust for danger he was a pleasure she was grateful to indulge in time and time again.

"So your product will be ready for pick up next month," Christopher said into the phone before hanging up. "What's your issue?" he asked Maria angrily.

"I want you to take me somewhere?" she said.

"This is my busy season. What the fuck you want a vacation?" Christopher shouted throwing the phone on the table before sitting down across from her. "I'm going out of town next week anyway. I'll be gone for a day or two at most,"

"Can I come?" she whispered.

"It's business," he snapped.

"Dangerous business?" she asked and he looked at her with an attitude. "If you're going somewhere dangerous I want you to take extra security with you,"

"I can't afford anymore security," he grunted.

"Baby, you're stressed and I get that. But I need assurances that you will be okay," Maria said getting up from her chair to walk over to him.

"Assurances, why the hell do you need assurances?" he asked as she sat on his lap.

"This is your castle, you're protected here. But with you gone who'll protect me,"

"I pay Ambrogino to protect you," Christopher said trying to look tough as he placed his hands on her body. She took a deep breath, placing her hand on his chest. Her eyes darting between his eyes and his lips as she leaned closer.

"I'm pregnant," she said. Christopher, looking overjoyed shook his head.

"No shit," he said and she nodded her head. "Yeah, you're pregnant!?" he asked again giving her a kiss before she had time to answer.

"I want you safe, I need you safe," she said with tears in her eyes.

"Okay, if it'll make you feel better I'll hire a few more guys," he said.

"You don't have to. I've already sent Ambrogino to get some people that he trusts. Throw away guys, so you don't have to pay when you're done." she said.

"You had this shit planned all along didn't you, Baby?" he asked. She nodded her head slightly, smiling back before kissing him.

"I love you so much," she whispered in his ear.

"I need a drink," he said shaking his head, still in disbelief.

9

While in the principal's office Aparicio, Ridha and Kolya stood before Mr. Quwan and principle Richart. At the age of 21 their bodies personified the definition of perfection and their mental state unbreakable.

"You three have come a long way in the years you have been here. You have survived uncanny obstacles and gained the experience that no other soldier in the world could have in one lifetime." Principle Richart said pouring himself a cup of scotch for Mr. Quwan and himself. "But you have yet to graduate," he said handing a cup to Mr. Quwan. As the two men clinked glasses and took a sip Mr. Quwan turned to them.

"Men, tomorrow you will be tested. If you survive then you will be welcomed into the Order, the highest honor we can bestow to anyone." he said finishing the scotch in his glass.

"Sleep well," Mr. Richart said with a smile. Walking around the desk he shook each of their hands. "When you three survive the test I expect to hear a great many things from my superiors. For many, many years to come." that being said they were dismissed to their rooms to get as much shut eye as they could.

Four hours later members from the Order of Flame, dressed in all black, burst into each of their rooms. Before Kolya and Ridha could jump out of bed they were shot with tranquilizer darts. When they burst into Aparicio's room they fired into an empty bed. As the three men narrowed their eyes Aparicio leapt from the corner of the room punching one of them in the stomach so hard they keeled over gasping for air. The other two turned and immediately began swinging their fists in his direction. Aparicio countered with a flurry of jabs, punches and kicks but he was out matched and being forced back.

When his back reached the wall, Aparicio, he cart wheeled out of the way forcing one of the men to punch the wall with all his might. As the other turned to pursue, Aparicio, punched him in the throat before hearing the sound of a dart gun go off. Turning quickly he saw the first man he had punched had taken his time, reloaded, aimed and fired off a shot the reached its target. His right arm. The others he had just been dealing with stopped and stared as Aparicio tried to fight the drug now coursing though his body. Slowly he knelt down and smiled at them before collapsing into unconsciousness.

When Aparicio's eyes fluttered open he knew there was a bag over his head, his arms and legs bound. The sounds of an engine echoed around him, giving him a splitting headache. Then the bag was removed and Mr. Quwan was standing over him.

"Wake up soldier, this is not a drill!" he shouted but his words still seemed muffled and the image of him looked blurred as the tranquilizer was wearing off. Looking to his left he saw Kolya and Ridha looking in no better shape than he.

"In two minutes your test begins so listen up," Mr. Quwan said as they each tried to get their bearings. "Strapped to your backs are parachutes. This is something we've never taught you how to use so once you leave count to twenty then pull the red cord. Count to twenty than pull the red cord!" he shouted to reinforce his words in their scattered heads.

"I've never done this," Kolya said looking sick.

"That's the point!" Mr. Quwan said grabbing Kolya by the back of the head. "Don't interrupt!" he screamed letting him go. When you reach the forest your orders are to seize and capture six Seal Team commandos. Capture, do not kill!"

"We can't kill them?" Ridha asked feeling confused.

"Anyone can kill, Soldier. Now your job is to capture. When all of them are captured it is your job to find the city where you will receive new orders. Do we understand one another gentlemen?!" Mr. Quwan shouted.

"Yes, Sir!" they answered in unison. Mr. Quwan gave them a moment as they forced themselves through the sedative coursing through their bodies. It was Ridha who first realized where they were and stood up.

"Sir, we're on a plane?!" he shouted looking down to realize he was in the Order of Flame gear.

Mr. Quwan smiled and slammed his fist into a red button on the wall behind him. A door slowly opened and wind began rushing in making all conversation useless. Mr. Quwan removed a combat knife from Kolya's boot and tossed it out the plane. He then grabbed the goggles on Ridha's head and lowered them. The goggles revealed the plane's interior in a bright green. Ridha shook his head as Mr. Quwan shoved him out of the plane.

"We are bound," Kolya said as Mr. Quwan helped him to his feet. "How are we to free ourselves when you throw us out a plane bound!?" he screamed but his voice might as well have been mute as the wind made it difficult for Kolya to hear his own voice. As Mr. Quwan threw Kolya out the plane he read Kolya's lips as he screamed. "Fuck this shit!"

As Mr. Quwan turned to grab Aparicio he noticed the boy was gone. Glancing around the back of the plane until his sixth sense began to flare, he turned and saw Aparicio standing at the edge of the plane's hangar looking back at him, his restraints gone. With a nod, Aparicio put his goggles on and jumped.

"Go get 'em kid," Mr. Quwan said closing the hatch.

Ridha didn't have much time as he tried to locate the combat knife. When he got it in sight he aimed is body toward it, turning around for his hand to grab the knife just as he passed by. Cutting his wrist restraints loose he looked up and saw Kolya off in the distance. Once his arms were free, Ridha began working on his leg restraints all the while counting. Time was nearly up and there was no way to reach Kolya and pull the parachute cord.

As his restraints were cut loose Ridha threw the knife as best he could toward Kolya before pulling the parachute's red cord. With no way to see or grab the knife Kolya missed Ridha's intention, instead he felt someone slam into him, wrapping legs around his waist, then hands grabbing his face. As the goggles were placed over his head he noticed Aparicio cutting his wrist restraints off, then his leg restraints.

Giving Kolya a thumbs up, Aparicio pulled Kolya's red cord and pushed off as the parachute deployed. Kolya looked up and saw Aparicio getting some distance from him before deploying his parachute. As the group slowly descended down they noticed they were fast approaching tall trees. Instinctively they each held their breaths as they fell into the trees. As the parachutes became tangled in the branches they hung for a moment as each one caught their bearings.

"Everyone okay?" Ridha asked.

"Mr. Quwan wanted to kill me," Kolya grunted angrily as he looked around for his knife.

"Here," Aparicio said tossing Kolya's knife to him. "I found that on my way down," Before anyone cut themselves free they each surveyed the area.

"Okay we are in a forest," Ridha sighed.

"About a hundred feet in the air too," Aparicio added.

"And not one of us has a strong enough branch to support our weight going down," Kolya grunted.

"How many people are after us?" Ridha asked.

"Six I believe," Kolya said shaking his head. Aparicio removed his knife and began moving his body back and forth until he was swinging.

Removing his own boot knife, Aparicio, began cutting the parachute's cords. "I'll see you guys at the bottom," he said. While falling he was able to plant his feet on the side of one tree before pushing off to grab the branch of another. He then swung to a lower branch which broke under his weight. Kicking off a tree trunk, Aparicio, flipped backwards onto the side of another tree where he kicked off and landed in the mud beside the tree.

"He's such a showoff," Ridha said following Aparicio's lead. Kolya sneered as he began to follow Ridha. Once they were all safely on the ground they performed a weapons check.

"My Glock is out of ammo," Kolya said angrily.

"The mission is to capture, not kill." Aparicio said as he checked his pockets for a map or medical supplies.
Nothing.

"If we've got our bullet proof vests than that means that they can shoot to kill," Ridha sighed.

"Okay, we need to camouflage ourselves then. I remember Mr. Quwan saying that we had to capture Navy Seals," Aparicio said and the group agreed. Each of them removed their black hooded sweaters and their beige khakis and began rolling them in the mud to conceal their colors. Then they tore shrubs and leaves, placing them on their clothes before disappearing into the fog that was sweeping into the forest.

"They landed here," a man in full combat gear said into a radio. Next to him were three others who positioned themselves around to secure the area.

"They scattered in four directions," another man said looking at the different foot prints.

"Orders say there are three of them," the first man said looking around the thick fog. "I think they're trying to bait us into thinking there are four," the men kept sharp eyes on the area but with the fog it was hard for their minds not to play tricks on them. All the while Ridha hid in the mud beside them, covered by the fog.

"Let's keep going but maintain radio silence," a voice came back from over the radio. As the men marched onward they left Ridha behind as well as three maps, three extra ammo clips, three radios and three packs of medical supplies. When the cost was clear Ridha stood up, gathered what he stole and kept moving. Once Ridha met up with the others they divided the bounty and split up once more.

Following signs where the forest had been disturbed the four military men continued to crawl through the mud for nearly two hours before they stopped. The first man radioed in his position but received no answer.

"Base do you copy?" he asked into his radio but all that came back was static.

"You don't think they got to the base do you?" one of the other men asked.

"Let's double time it back, we've gone too far out." the first man said. As they turned to run back Kolya jumped from behind a tree grabbing the last soldier by the mouth, his other hand rendering him unconscious, before dropping him into the fog. Kolya then fired two rounds into the trees near the Navy Seals to grab their attention.

Instinctively they each turned and opened fire. The two that led the march turned to cover their flank when rope from a parachute fell from the trees and landed around their necks like a noose. The men instinctively grabbed the rope around their necks, their other hands aiming upward to shoot the line. Before they could get a round off, Kolya, ran forward and grabbed their guns before disappearing behind a tree. When their oxygen was depleted and their eyes closed, faces turning purple, they were dropped to the ground. Their bodies fell to floor making a thud sound as the fog slowly moved around them. All that was left was the first man who had talked into his radio.

"Where the fuck are you mother fuckers!" he screamed, the deafening sound of his voice was all that he could hear in the forest around him. He turned around in a circle, seeing the bodies of his men as they were slowly swallowed by the fog. "Fight, fight me like a man you scared little shits!" he screamed opening fire with his M16 assault rifle but his ammunition clip was gone.

Throwing the rifle to the side he removed his side arm and knelt beside two of his men who looked as though they were strangled. When he checked their pulse he was relieved to see they were alive, unconscious, but alive. Taking a deep breath he tried slapping one of them awake when he felt the sting of cold steal in his thigh. Looking down he saw a throwing knife, hilt deep, in his left leg. Turning to fire in the direction it came from left his back exposed. Ridha quickly emerged from the fog and placed the soldier in a choke hold until he passed out. Once all the men were tied together Kolya looked at Ridha and smiled.

"Two more," Kolya said removing the soldier's radio.

"You think Aparicio's got them?" Ridha asked when the sound of white noise came from the radios. The two stared at one another and dove for cover before the bullet from a sniper rifle nearly split them in two.

"Sniper!" Kolya snapped as he crawled slowly through the mud, using the fog as cover. When Ridha didn't answer Kolya shook his head, had he already forgotten everything he had learned. Finding a branch that lay in the mud he removed his bullet proof vest. Placing the vest on the branch, he hoisted it in the air near a tree. Edging it out slowly he waited to see if the sniper would take the bait. Another shot fired and a chunk from the tree splintered off, the vest falling onto the ground beside Kolya.

"I've got his position," Ridha said, throwing his voice to Kolya when two more shots went off. Looking around they both noticed that the shots recently fired weren't in their direction.

"We must hurry," Kolya said, if the shots fired weren't aimed at them than Aparicio must have been spotted. As they made their way through the fog the Navy Seals radio came to life.

"Are you okay?" Aparicio's voice said. Ridha picked up his radio and answered in Morse code.

"We meet in the middle," Aparicio said over the radio, code, which meant they should meet where they first landed. As the men gathered beneath their parachutes trapped in the trees above they greeted one another with high fives and handshakes.

"You took care of their base?" Ridha asked.

"They had three people at their base camp. I pulled a tear gas grenade from one and took them out. Luckily the sniper took a shot at you two and I caught a glimpse from my position," Aparicio said dusting leaves from his shoulder.

"Any intelligence from their base camp?" Kolya asked as he helped Aparicio remove as much camouflage from his sweater as possible.

"We're in Mount Sutro Forest, not far from the city." Aparicio said.

"What's 'not far' mean?" Ridha had questioned brushing the mud from his khakis. Aparicio pulled out his map and handed it to Ridha.

"From what I can tell maybe an hour run?" he said pointing to their position.

"Then what, we have no new orders." Kolya asked.

"We can figure that out once we get to the city. What we need now is food, these military rations won't last long," Ridha said folding the map back.

"I saw some tire treads near the Seals base," Aparicio said looking around to see if they were being watched. "Maybe we can hitch a ride and clean these clothes. Blend into society and take it from there," he said with a shrug of his shoulders.

"Yeah," Kolya agreed and just before Ridha could voice his oppinion he noticed the smile on Aparicio's face.

"You know something we don't," Ridha said shaking his head. Aparicio nodded, reaching into his pocket to pull out three wallets. "I took these just in case. We've got a total of six credit cards and seventy five dollars in cash,"

"Let's go," Kolya said punching Aparicio in the arm before running off.

"Were you going to tell us?" Ridha asked him.

"Eventually," Aparicio answered as the two of them jogged after Kolya.

10

When they reached the makeshift base the Navy Seals had set up in the forest, Aparicio, began looking for the tire tracks he saw earlier. Ridha and Kolya looked at the bullet riddled trees and damaged radio equipment.

"I thought you got the drop on them," Kolya said but Aparicio ignored him completely.

"Where are the Seals?" Ridha asked when he saw two men tied to a tree in the distance. "Why did you tie them up over there?"

"Found the tracks," Aparicio said walking back to the group. "I separated them so I could gather intelligence. When they refused to talk I placed them together and kept moving," Aparicio said waving for them to follow him. After a twelve minute sprint through the woods they came to a clearing where a black SUV was waiting.

"I'll drive," Kolya said, more as a statement than a question, pushing past them. Cautiously they approached the SUV, when everything looked clear Kolya busted the driver side window and opened the door. Ridha and Aparicio kept a look out while

Kolya scanned the car for listening devices, bombs and tracking devices.

"We're clean," he said cracking the bottom of the steering column away to reveal colored wires. Seconds later they were driving through the dirt path toward San Francisco.

When they found a normal road just outside the forest the SUV's GPS system activated giving them a route.

"Do you suppose that's what our next objective is?" Ridha asked.

"Yes," Kolya said following the GPS directions while Aparicio rested in the back. The route took them to Vallejo Street before giving them a new set of coordinates.

"Should we?" Kolya questioned as they all looked around the area from the SUV.

"No time like the present," Aparicio said getting out the SUV. Cautiously they walked to the address the SUV had asked them to stop. 1425 Vallejo, a three story building with a built in garage. Aparicio stepped out and took a glance at the mail box and noticed his name.

"Do you think this is your home?" Kolya asked. Ridha took a deep breath before looking up at the sky which was now turning from black to a slightly lighter shade.

"We have maybe an hour of daylight left. The GPS has another address, I'm thinking this is your new home," Ridha said.

"Room 306," Aparicio said reading the number next to his name. The group walked into the building and made their way to the apartment. Opening the door slowly they were pleasantly surprised to see a fully furnished, spacious, loft.

"Nice," Ridha whispered as everyone removed their Glock .26 pistols and entered the house. After checking every room the group gathered in the living room, Aparicio smiling ear to ear.

"You guys check out your homes, shower, get some sleep and lets all meet back here in say twelve hours?" Aparicio asked.

"Sounds good," Kolya said patting him on the shoulder. "See you soon,"

"Take care," Ridha said putting his gun away. As the group left, Aparicio, began shedding his dirty clothes as he made his way to the refrigerator. When he opened the door he noticed the refrigerator was packed with various fruits and vegetables, bottle waters and organic juices. Grabbing an apple he began opening the cabinets to see the various amounts of cereal.

"Life is good," he said with a smile.

As Kolya and Ridha left they followed the GPS to 1245 Scott St. nearly twenty five minutes away with light traffic. Once they reached the building Ridha and Kolya walked toward the address list and noticed Ridha's name was displayed.

"Would you like me to go inside with you?" Kolya asked.

"No I got this. Go see where your place is, I'm guessing not too far from here. I'll see you in about eleven and a half hours," Kolya nodded his head and walked back to the car, waiting outside the home until Ridha had been in the apartment for more than five minutes. Upon entering Ridha noticed the lay out was very similar to Aparicio's place. Rather than checking the refrigerator, Ridha, swept the place before going to the shower where he shed his clothes to take a much needed shower.

Kolya followed the GPS to 55 O' Farrell Street. His new home seemed to be above a clothing store. The entire area looked to be a large shopping spot with multiple stores and restaurants. Parking the car he made his way to the doorway on the side of the clothing store. Taking the stairs to his new apartment he ignored the layout and the refrigerator, walking straight to the bedroom where he noticed queen size bed with a manila envelope waiting for him.

"Should I?" he questioned but his desire for sleep outweighed his curiosity. Taking the envelope he tossed it to the side of the bed along with his dirty clothes. Jumping on the bed he took a deep breath, exhaling slowly while closing his eyes, drifting off to sleep.

When 6:22p.m came Aparicio heard a knock on his door. He quickly ran to the door wearing blue jeans and a red t-shirt. Upon opening the door he saw Ridha wearing blue jeans with a white shirt while Kolya had shorts and a black t-shirt.

"This sure beats those sweat clothes we had to wear," he said standing aside for them to enter.
"How are your apartments?"

"The same layout," Kolya said walking to the plush leather couch.

"Yeah, did you two get the manila envelopes on your bed?" Ridha asked following Aparicio to the kitchen where they both retrieved a bottle of water.

"Kolya, you want some water?" Aparicio asked but when Kolya declined he and Ridha walked back to the living room to sit.

"Yeah I got mine," Aparicio said.

"I didn't get to open mine," Kolya admitted.

"Too bad," Ridha laughed. "They had some nice things in there,"

"Like?"

"I had two grand in cash," Aparicio said. "A couple of credit cards, passports, ID's and a map of the area,"

"Same, but I had the note too," Ridha agreed.

"Note?" Kolya asked.

"Yeah," Aparicio said. "A note that said we were to lay low for a couple of days, blend in and wait until we're called for duty,"

"Oh and we have these," Ridha said pulling out a cell phone.

"We have phones now!" Kolya said jumping up.

"Yeah they have our number pre-programmed into them." Aparicio said as Kolya stood over Ridha to look at the phone.

"Pretty nice huh," Ridha said tossing it to Kolya.

"My first phone," Kolya whispered.

"MY first phone," Ridha corrected. "Yours is still in an envelope in your room." Aparicio and Ridha looked at Kolya while he admired the phone.

"So here we are. Three friends in a new city and completely off the clock," Aparicio said finishing off his water.

"I take it you're suggesting something?" Ridha asked.

"I say we paint the town red, pick up some dinner maybe check out the locals?"

"Yes please," Kolya said handing Ridha his phone back. "Maybe we can have sex," Kolya whispered prompting the others to laugh.

"Don't hold your breath," Aparicio said grabbing his keys. Ridha shook his head as he followed leaving Kolya to lower his head, blushing at the idea.

The walk around the area proved informative. Walking to Polk Street they found a few shopping stores and some decent restaurants. Ridha noticed a local book store and instinctively walked in to grab a map of the city. Kolya and Aparicio picked up a few books as well before grabbing their own maps. After a while they decided to double back toward the Starbucks on the corner of Vallejo and Polk St.

After a ten minute debate on what to have the Kolya decided to have coffee, Ridha asked for a bottle of water and a cookie while Aparicio ordered an ice coffee. Sitting down near a window to relax they passed around their book purchases and took quick glances at their maps. The group was silent as their peripheral vision counted the number of people coming in and out the cafe.

"When do you think our first assignment will be?" Kolya asked, his head constantly turning to keep one of the ladies behind the counter within view.

"Are you anxious to start working already?" Ridha asked in return while Aparicio's eyes stayed glued to the back of the books he bought.

"We have trained all of our young lives to be here, right here and now we have no direction. We have no guidance and we have no way of going back to the school. Complete freedom is now ours and I have no idea what to do with it," Kolya laughed but all eyes turned to Aparicio when he scoffed at Kolya's remark.

"You know what you want Kolya, all of us know. Why not try your luck with the lady behind the counter rather than stalking her from across the room,"

"That's not why we're here," Ridha interjected. "We're suppose to lay low and blend in with society until we are called,"

"That's just it Ridha," Kolya said taking a sip of his coffee. "We are completely free to do as we please, we were trained to be magnificent in just about everything we do. Why not use this skill to just disappear." Kolya then offered his coffee to Ridha to try. Ridha shook his head and when Kolya turned to Aparicio he noticed his head was still buried in the books he bought.

"You know what they will do if they found out we ran," Ridha said.

"I've heard rumors but that's all they were," Kolya said putting his coffee down to look at some of the books he had bought.

"The night Arthur burst into my room they sent someone like us in to break up the fight. There are more than likely hundreds of others like us, specially trained to keep us in line should one or all of us decide to disappear," Aparicio said looking up from his books to lean back in his chair. "Running isn't an option guys. We're in this to the end," he said taking a sip of his ice coffee.

"I understand that but if one had the opportunity to disappear, where would you go?" Ridha asked with a playful smile. As they expected, Kolya was all too eager to let them know where he wanted to go.

"I would like to go back to Russia and see my sister again. I can only imagine what she would say if she knew what has become of my life. Then I would like to find my family. What about you?" Kolya asked Ridha specifically.

"Wow," Ridha said with a laugh. "My parents were killed in front of me by government officials. I spent a month rummaging through alleys to survive until I was picked up by the school. But to answer your question, I've always thought of traveling to America. My parents would often call it the land of Milk and Honey."

Kolya placed a heavy hand on Ridha's shoulders.

"And now you are here my friend. Do you have any brothers and sisters?" Ridha sighed when Kolya asked the question, his eyes almost shedding a tear at the thought.

"My brothers were working with the government officials who killed them," Ridha then turned to Aparicio who had been shaking his head in disbelief.

"You wouldn't want to go back?" Kolya asked. "Ask them why they did it, get vengeance?"

"We all have our demons Kolya. Sometimes they're just better left buried in the past," Aparicio said looking over at Ridha who was now fully composed.

"Share with us, Brother, what secrets do you have?" Kolya asked. Ridha and Kolya stared at Aparicio for a moment as he quickly debated telling him his story.

"I buried it so deep I don't even know it anymore," Aparicio answered.

"Nothing stays buried forever friend," Ridha whispered.

"Brothers, sisters, mother?" Kolya asked and Aparicio's eyes went into a daze as he tried to recall his past.

"Its strange." he began trying to remember his life so long ago. "I don't remember names or faces anymore. I never knew my mother or father but I remember being very fond of a girl. I remember what it was like to be betrayed and what it felt like to be alone," Aparicio said looking back between the two. "My past is irrelevant, all of ours are. The Order took us in when we were nothing, they loved us when no one else would and they gave us a trade unlike any other. I think we'd be fools to just walk away from them. Shit, the consequences for disloyalty are worse than death."

A silence fell on the group as they pondered what Aparicio had said.

"You're right," Ridha said after a moment of reflection. "The past shall stay buried,"

"To the future," Kolya said raising his coffee cup. The others raised their cups in agreement.

"Yes," Ridha agreed.

11

Ambrogino waited outside the San Francisco international airport with a single suitcase until a white limousine arrived to retrieve him. Upon entering the limo he was greeted by a man sitting opposite of him wearing a gray suit, his face shrouded by the darkness of the cabin.

"Drink?" the shrouded man asked, while holding a crystal glass with, what smelled like, a scotch in his right hand.

"No thank you," Ambrogino answered placing his suitcase on the seat beside him.

"Straight to the point, I can respect that." the man replied taking a sip of the scotch.

"My employer will be picking up a cargo container in six days from the docks here in San Francisco. I'd like it very much if he didn't survive the trip back to Miami." Ambrogino said.

"Who's your employer?"

"His name is Christopher Fraga. He runs-"

"A significant part of Miami's underground circuit. We know who he is," the shrouded man said nodding his head. "Killing him will upset a delicate balance that has been put in place in Miami. Killing him will be costly,"

"A delicate balance?"

"Yes Mr. Colombo. Christopher Fraga is in power because we put him there," the man said and suddenly Ambrogino could feel a cold tingling sensation down his spine. If what he was saying was true then he had just asked to have the man they wanted running part of Miami killed. "You can relax Mr. Colombo, just because we put him there doesn't mean we can't put someone else in his place. But if you want him dead then I can only surmise that you have someone ready to do the job,"

Ambrogino nodded his head, no longer feeling comfortable with his situation, using his peripheral vision to keep track of where the limo was going. Unfortunately the limo driver had taken the expressway and was going too fast for him to jump out the car and tumble to safety.

"Her name is Maria. Christopher Fraga's fiancé," there was a moment of silence.

"We can do the job for ten million. Five now, five upon completion but we will need information and assurances," the man said finishing off his scotch.

"What kind of assurances?" Ambrogino asked, his right hand tapping the top of his thigh.

"Christopher Fraga's fiance' stays in Miami. No expanding for at least two years,"

"What happens after two years have passed?"

"She's free to expand or not expand, it doesn't matter. We have certain assets in place outside of Miami and if she does not stay within her territory it could disrupt the balance of things," the shrouded man said crossing his legs.

"And if she expands before the two years and disrupts your delicate balance what happens, you kill her entire operation?" Ambrogino asked feeling as though he already knew the answer.

"No Mr. Colombo. We make her, you, and anyone in her entire organization disappear and replace all of you with someone else. Someone more than willing to play by the rules,"

"What information do you require?"

"When will Mr. Fraga be in town, exactly," the shrouded man asked.

"He arrives the day before on Saturday. He'll be with an entourage of six or seven men. As well as his personal body guard Angela. The following day at 2a.m he picks up his merchandise. A container marked, 8178. The window of opportunity ends at 3a.m." Ambrogino explained.

"What happens after 3am?"

"MS-13 gang members come in to pick up their own shipment. Christopher can't afford any complications from dock workers getting suspicions about the transaction. So he has to hitch the cargo container to a truck and start the drive back to Miami."

"We need to know what's in the cargo container,"

"Why?" Ambrogino shot back.

"We're professionals Mr. Colombo. A ton of time, money and resources go into training our people. If something in this container leaks, explodes or hisses out into the atmosphere, I need to know that my people are safe and that no attention will be brought to them, or you." this time Ambrogino sighed. "Mr. Colombo, you came to us because we have no record of our existence. We're but a whisper on the wind in a very large and extremely noisy world. Now you can contemplate going for the wooden knife you smuggled through airport security," Ambrogino looked shocked when he heard him mention the wooden knife in his boot.

"What?"

"You might even gamble your life by jumping out of this vehicle to try your luck on the expressway but all sane options point to you and I concluding our business and you going home,"

"I don't even know your name," Ambrogino said out of spite.

"You're not supposed to know me Mr. Colombo but if you must have a name you can call me Mr. Dark." he said. "What's in the container?"

"It's my understanding that it's women,"

"Slave trafficking women has never been Mr. Fraga's thing in the past. Are you sure?" Mr. Dark asked his tone of voice very forceful.

"Mr. Fraga has plans on expanding outside of Miami. From what I was told he's got some Indians coming in and he wants to impress them with some Russian escorts. Clean ones that he could turn around and use as prostitutes." Another moment of silence passed.

"Do you know the name of the ship?"

"No,"

"Does it matter if Mr. Fraga's entourage is killed during the exchange?"

"I would prefer it if they were left alone but I understand if there is collateral damage,"

"Mr. Colombo we don't believe in collateral damage. Do you want the container once he's dead?"

"Preferably yes,"

"Then I do believe we have a deal. Once Mr. Fraga is dead an agent will arrive at his home to collect the final payment. Should I have them ask for you or Maria?" Mr. Dark asked.

"They can ask for me," Ambrogino said.

"Excellent. Just as a formality, should something go wrong on our part we will refund your money and then some as well as finish the job. Should something go wrong on yours, there is nowhere on this planet that we cannot find you," Ambrogino nodded his head.

"Here is your five million," he said pushing the suit case onto the floor.

"Excellent," Mr. Dark said. "Where can we drop you off?"

Ambrogino was dropped off at the airport where he immediately made his way to the VIP lounge. Once inside he walked to one of the comfy chairs in the secluded room and pulled out his cell phone. His first inclination was to call Maria but thought best to send a text first.

R U Busy?
He waited for nearly ten minutes before he received a reply.

With Christopher, contact you when it's safe
Closing his phone he stood up and made his way to the nearest ticket counter where he booked a first class flight back to Miami. Since his flight would not leave for another three hours, Ambrogino had lunch and took some time to browse through magazines. After making a few purchases he was on his way to the VIP lounge when he felt his phone vibrate in his pocket. As he slid the phone out of his pocket his eyes glanced around to see if anyone was paying him any attention.

He glanced at the caller ID and saw that it was Maria returning his call. He placed the phone to his ear while making his way back to the VIP Lounge. As was routine both he and Maria waited ten seconds before speaking, to make sure no one was tapping the phone.

"Christopher was feeling frisky," Maria said after the ten seconds of silence.

"I placed an order for the job, everything is set." Ambrogino said in a light hearted tone in case someone within ear shot became interested in his conversation.

"Excellent, when do you return?" she asked, her voice sounding seductive.

"My flight leaves in a couple hours. I should be with you before dawn,"

"I'm dripping with the thought of you crawling into my bed as I'm asleep." she replied just as Ambrogino was entering the VIP lounge.

"I have to ask you something," his tone became deadly serious killing her mood.

"What happened?"

"I was asked detailed questions about the cargo coming in. Are we sure it's nothing more than Russian prostitutes?"

"Yes, I overheard Christopher talking to one of the Indians earlier today about two in particular. At least that's what I thought. Why?"

"They know that bringing Russian prostitutes into the country isn't something that he does. I think it's raised a red flag. They were also clear that the business cannot expand for a minimum of two years once this job is completed." he said taking a seat in a secluded area of the VIP room.

"Once this job is done I don't plan on expanding. I'm going to be too busy rebuilding our new empire," she said with a laugh. "I'll inquire about what is in the container. If we're lucky maybe it's something that could be advantageous to us," she said.

"No, I think its best that I do the inquiring. I'll see you when I reach Miami,"

12

Kolya, Aparicio and Ridha arrived at an abandoned warehouse separately after being summoned through a letter in the mail. The letter only giving a time and address with the initials L.G. Kolya, having searched the area around the warehouse first, walked in through the front door. As he entered, being careful not to make a noise, he noticed a fiber optic cable poking through a narrow grate on the floor. Before he could react the cable retracted and the grate was pushed outward and gently placed on the ground. Kolya already knew it would be Ridha before seeing his body wiggle out of the narrow hole in the ground. Looking upward he saw Aparicio on a support beam creeping out of a shadow.

Most of the warehouse's interior was bathed in shadows, making it difficult to know if there were others waiting for their arrival. Ridha placed the grate back before walking backward into one of the shadows to be unseen by the naked eye. Kolya stepped opposite Ridha and crouched down into the darkness when the warehouse door slid completely open bathing half of the interior in sunlight.

In the doorway stood a short but stocky silhouette that stood silent for a moment. The door closed soon after, the sound of footsteps echoing throughout the building until it stopped at a table near the back of the building.

"It's clear guys. Feel free to drop down." The man said removing a briefcase from under the table and it atop. When no one answered the man let out a sigh while opening the suitcase. "I don't have all day!" he shouted in anger when a large hand wrapped around his face. Shocked at the sudden attack the man through his head back to catch his assailant off guard but instead he fell into his arms which tightened around him.

"Who are you?" Kolya asked when the man reached for the back of his belt to retrieve a metal baton. Extending the baton with a flick of his wrist he threw it back catching Kolya in the head. The hit was powerful enough to make Kolya lose his grip but not powerful enough to draw blood. Turning around the man raised the baton as if to strike again. Kolya reached forward instinctively to grab his wrist when the man used his free hand to chop down on the side of Kolya's neck.

Wincing in pain Kolya dropped to one knee before getting kicked in the face.

The man then swung the baton around to swat a throwing needle intended for his head.

"Enough rookies!" the man screamed. "I'm your liaison for the Order!"

"How do we know you're telling the truth?" Ridha asked from the shadows. The man smirked as he looked around the darkened corners of the warehouse. He knew one was on the floor behind him, one was somewhere in the rafters above and the other...had to be hidden in the shadows somewhere.

"I sent you all letters. Letters to each of your homes, how the hell would I know to do that unless I knew who each of you are, Rookies." he scoffed.

"Why did you summon us?" Kolya asked while standing up and dusting himself off.

"The Order had an assignment for you," the man said.

Aparicio dropped from the ceiling and walked toward the table to reveal himself. "What is the assignment?" Aparicio asked. The man shook his head when he noticed Aparicio was dressed in full gear with his hood covering his face. Looking back he saw Kolya wearing the same outfit, his hood also covering his face.

"Not so simple," the man said looking back at Kolya. "They said the big one was Kolya, so I'm assuming that's you." the man said before turning his attention to Aparicio. "Which makes you either Ridha or Apar...something." he said unable to pronounce Aparicio.

"And you are?" Aparicio asked.

"Lamont Gibson. I'm the San Francisco handler for the Order." Aparicio noticed the man was well dressed in a white suit with a black shirt and a half black half white tie. His hair was low and neat much like the rest of him. Lamont's eyes shifted when he noticed Ridha stepping out of the shadows dressed like the others.

"Good now that we're all here I can go over my rules," Lamont said walking toward the table.

"Your rules?" Kolya asked. "We do not answer to you my black friend," Kolya grunted. Lamont placed the baton on the table next to his brief case and Aparicio automatically glanced down at Lamont's hands which had permanent scars from years of fighting.

"Was that a black joke Russian?" Lamont asked turning around to meet Kolya face to face.

"Orders be damned, I'll whoop yo' ass here and now if you don't show me some mother fucking respect, Bitch," Lamont snapped.

"Do not test me," Kolya said in protest.

"Stand down," Aparicio said but neither of them looked ready to back away from one another.

"Kolya, I said stand down!" Aparicio shouted.

"You can't win this Kolya," Ridha said. "Look down." Kolya looked down between them and saw Lamont had a blade between them, ready to cut open his lower stomach. His intestine would spill out and he'd be dead in minutes. Kolya gritted his teeth and swallowed his pride before nodding in defeat.

"I've been a member of the Order for a very long time. Most don't get to live as long as I do, so when I speak you best choose to listen. Get your Russian ass over to the table so I can give my welcome speech," Lamont ordered and much to everyone's surprise Kolya listened. Once they all stood side by side Lamont put his knife away.

"Here are the rules. No getting caught, EVER! You get caught you best find a way to escape or kill yourself. Rescue is not something we do in the Order. If I need you I will find you, don't bother looking for me because like the three of you I don't exist. My purpose is to give you the assignments given to me by the Order, your job is to carry it out to the letter. Do a job well, you get rewarded, do a job sloppy or fail to meet its objective...get dead. I don't like killing my brothers and sisters but I will if you don't play by the rules. And finally I don't like hearing anything about anyone being in the news. Any questions," Lamont asked and when Kolya opened his mouth Lamont shouted.

"Good, on to your first assignment," Aparicio smiled while Ridha widened his eyes as Kolya shuttered off his anger.

"Christopher Fraga is your target, he arrives in San Francisco in a week with an entourage of people." Lamont pulled a few photographs of Christopher from his briefcase to spread out on the table.

"We believe he's picking up a container of prostitutes from the docks here to impress some people back in his hometown of Miami. Kill him at the docks, make it look like something other than a group of assassins came to kill him." Lamont pulled out photos of the docks as well as the name of the ship bringing the girls and the cargo container number.

"That's it?" Ridha asked. "Just kill him,"

"Yeah," Lamont answered.

"We can choose how to do this?" Aparicio asked.

"So long as it gets done," Lamont responded.

"What if we need special equipment?" Aparicio asked while staring at the photos of the docks. Lamont smirked.

"You must be Apa something, they said you were the cleaver one." Lamont scoffed.

"Apa-Ree-Cee-Oh," Aparicio said sounding out his name to Lamont who looked unimpressed.

"What do you think you might need?"

"Something to jam communications," Kolya said and Ridha agreed.

"Yeah, I can rig a small laptop to send a jamming signal large enough to blanket the area. This way we could contain the people," Ridha said looking at the photo of the docks.

"The ship is Russian, since the mob operates here perhaps we could use it to our advantage if things do not go according to plan," Kolya added. When Aparicio did not say anything Lamont began to stare at him.

"Well genius, what's going through your mind?" Lamont asked.

"We can't just walk in and kill him. We either have to be there a day before they arrive or come in after the ship has docked." Aparicio said.

"True, but if we hide there a day before we could get caught, by security," Ridha said.

"We'll have to swim to the docks. We put our gear in our bags, stay under the water until after the ship docks." Aparicio said.

"Okay, good thinking." Lamont said. "Then you complete the contract and leave."

"We put C4 on the ship, make it look like Christopher double crossed the Russians. A fight breaks out and Christopher gets caught in the crossfire."

"What?" Lamont said seeing the plan falling apart.

"Why destroy the ship?" Kolya asked.

"They're trafficking women and more than likely they're also trafficking drugs and guns. Why not bring the whole thing down?" Aparicio said.

"Because that's not the job," Lamont snapped.

"The fire fight will cause too much attention," Ridha whispered.

"I'd be willing to bet that we could kill Christopher before a fire fight broke out, blow the ship and then let them start the firefight on their own." Aparicio said with a smirk.

"I don't like this plan. Too many flaws already but if that's what you rookies want to go with then that's on you. Just remember that I don't like cleaning up a mess," Lamont said putting the pictures back in the brief case. "I'll have the necessary equipment delivered to one of your homes." Lamont said pulling out a match book.

"The laptop?" Ridha asked.

"I said I'll have the necessary equipment delivered to one of your homes," Lamont then tossed the match into the brief case lighting the pictures on fire. "You won't see me again until I summon you back here after the mission." he said as the fire began to rise. Kolya and Ridha nodded while Aparicio pondered the plan in his head once more.

"Go do your recon, think the mission over a little more. Make sure to cross all your T's and dot all those I's. See you when it's over," he said walking away.

"I think we should just kill them silently, why stage an entire gun fight if we don't need to?" Kolya asked.

"It's our first assignment Kolya. Don't you want to add a little flare, get noticed by the Order?" Aparicio replied.

"No, this kind of action could get us killed." Kolya responded angrily.

"You did plenty of that on your own buddy," Ridha laughed. Kolya shook his head, feeling more embarrassment than anger.

"Who wants to do recon on Christopher?" Aparicio asked and Ridha was all too eager to raise his hand.

"I would like to check the docks out once more," Kolya said.

"You sure?" Aparicio asked and Kolya nodded. "You want me to come with?"

"I prefer to do this alone," Kolya said walking away.

"How about we get together at my place in two days then?" Aparicio asked. Ridha nodded while Kolya waved him off.

To be continued

**Unique 2017
By
Rick Torres**

Printed in Dunstable, United Kingdom